THERE'S A
DRAGON
IN MY
DI____R!

For Kaye and Erin.

In memory of my wonderful mum,
Diana Horne, the funniest person
I ever knew – S.H.

STRIPES PUBLISHING
An imprint of Little Tiger Press
1 The Coda Centre, 189 Munster Road,
London SW6 6AW

A paperback original
First published in Great Britain in 2016

Text copyright © Tom Nicoll, 2016
Illustrations copyright © Sarah Horne, 2016
Author photograph © Kaye Nicoll, 2016

ISBN: 978-1-84715-671-6

THERE'S A
DRAGON
IN MY
DINNER!

TOM NICOLL

ILLUSTRATED BY
SARAH HORNE

CHAPTER 1
A CHANGE OF FORTUNE

"Hey, Eric," said the tiny short-haired girl standing outside my front door. Min Song and I were in the same class at school, but right now she was here on official business, which was why she was carrying a dozen Chinese takeaway boxes under her chin. "Sorry we're so late."

"Er ... we ordered five minutes ago," I said, checking my watch.

"I know, I know, but traffic was a nightmare," she said, nodding towards her dad who was sitting on a moped with the words "Panda Cottage" emblazoned on the side, impatiently tapping his watch.

"No, what I meant was—" But before I could finish Min had shoved the huge pile of boxes into my arms.

Then she picked up a box that had fallen to the ground. "Oh, and don't forget your beansprouts."

"Beansprouts?" I said, looking puzzled. "I don't think we ordered—"

"No, they're free," interrupted Min. "We have *way* too many of them. Please, just take it."

"Oh, OK," I said. "You know, I've never actually tried them."

"You'll love them. Probably. Anyway, I have to go."

I put down the boxes and handed her the money, before she hopped on the moped and it disappeared down the road.

"Min took her time!"

That's my dad, Monty Crisp. He's the reason we were having a Friday-night Chinese. My dad manages the local football team, the Kippers, and we were celebrating their latest success – a 10–1 scoreline.

"I still can't believe it," he said as I handed him the boxes. "We got an actual goal. First time in five years. All right, so technically it was the other team that scored it for us, but an own goal still counts!"

Sorry, I should have been more clear: They *lost* 10–1.

The Kippers are the worst football team of all time. In their fifty-year history they've only ever won a single game, and even then it was because the other team had to forfeit after getting stuck in traffic.

"You should be very proud, dear," said my mum, Maya. In case you're wondering, her legs are currently over her head because she's a yoga instructor, not because she's weird. Though she is weird.

Mum unfolded herself and joined me, Dad, my two-and-a-half-year-old sister Posy and our horrible, definitely evil, cat Pusskin at the kitchen table.

Half an hour later, the Crisp family was officially stuffed, as you can see from my helpful diagram:

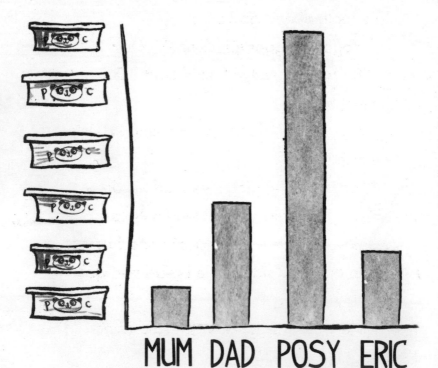

MUM DAD POSY ERIC

The number of boxes for Posy is misleading. Those are the number of *actual boxes* she attempted to eat. She doesn't bother about the food, she just loves chewing plastic.

After dinner, Dad was back talking sport.

"All I'm saying, Eric," he said, reaching for the fortune cookies, "is that it wouldn't kill you to take an interest in athletic pursuits. Like football or rugby or..."

"Yoga?" suggested Mum.

"Be serious, Maya," said Dad. "Er... I mean..."

Mum glared at him. "I'll pretend I didn't hear that."

Dad mimed wiping sweat off his brow. "Phew. But really, Eric, it was only last week you told me you thought offside was when only *one* side of the bread had gone mouldy..."

"He was *teasing*, Monty," said Mum.

"You *were* teasing him, weren't you, Eric?"

Before I could reply Dad cut in: "Hey, would you look at that?"

He held up a small piece of paper.

VICTORY WILL BE YOURS

"You beauty!" cried Dad. "It's destiny."

I rolled my eyes. "Everyone knows fortune cookies are rubbish, Dad. The last one I got said 'Your shoes will make you happy'."

"And did they?" Dad asked.

"Not that I noticed…"

"What did you get this time, Eric?" asked Mum.

I cracked open the shell and unfurled the piece of paper inside.

YOUR LIFE IS ABOUT TO CHANGE

"Hmm. Well, you do turn nine soon," Mum said.

"A week tomorrow," I reminded her. She *probably* knew that already, but my birthday was WAY too important to take any chances with.

"Ooh, look at mine," said Mum. "'Your son will handle the washing-up'."

"It doesn't say that," I said.

"Well, all right," she admitted. "It's actually the same as Dad's."

VICTORY WILL BE YOURS

"But you cleaning up will be a nice victory for me," she said.

I let out a groan, but I knew from experience that I had about as much chance of getting out of it as the Kippers did of winning, well ... anything.

I rinsed out all the boxes and took them outside. I'd almost finished putting them in the recycling bin when I realized that the box of beansprouts was still unopened.

Even though I was stuffed, I was curious to find out what they tasted like. I opened the lid and jumped back in fright. Not because of the beansprouts, though they didn't look that appetizing, but because nestled inside the box was a small green scaly object. It had:

A long dragon-like snout.

A long dragon-like tail.

Big dragon-like wings.

Sharp dragon-like teeth.

Short dragon-like arms and legs.

Dragon-like claws.

There was no doubt about it. Whatever it was looked a lot like a dragon. Its tiny marble-like black eyes seemed to stare back at me and, for the briefest of moments, I almost convinced myself it was real.

Ha. A real dragon. Can you imagine?

Were Panda Cottage giving out free toys with their food now?

"Snappy Meals," I said out loud, before remembering there was no one around to laugh at my joke.

I took the toy out of the box and was surprised by how it felt. Whatever it was made of, it wasn't plastic. I once touched a lizard at the zoo and it felt quite similar – rough and cool to the touch – but this was much, much harder. It really was the most lifelike toy I had ever seen. It must have taken forever to paint. Not that it even looked or felt painted, mind you. It was too realistic. Every scale was a different shade of green, with small, freckle-like flecks of yellow across the snout. Gently, I moved its arms and legs back and forth, feeling a little resistance as I did so, almost as if it didn't appreciate me doing it.

Whoever had made it must have gone to some trouble – way more than a free Chinese takeaway toy was worth, that's for sure.

After trying a handful of beansprouts and deciding I wasn't a fan, I shoved the dragon into my pocket, went back inside and headed upstairs. After all, it was Friday and I had a lot to do. My comics weren't going to read themselves.

I put the tiny dragon on a shelf before diving on to my bed and settling into issue #437 of my favourite comic: *Slug Man*.

A short while later, Slug Man was just about to take a call from the Police Commissioner on the Slug Phone when I felt something tugging at my trouser leg.

"Yeah?" I said, too absorbed in the story to bother looking down.

"What you reading?" said a childish voice.

"Oh, it's the latest issue of *Slug Man*," I replied.

"Any good?" asked the voice, which sounded like it had a Chinese accent.

"It's amazing," I said. "He's about to fight his arch-enemy, The Salt Shaker."

"Cool. I love comics. I mean, I haven't actually *read* any, but they look awesome."

"Help yourself," I said, still not taking my eyes off the page but pointing towards the pile at the side of my bed.

"Don't mind if I do. Thanks!"

"No worries," I said.

I continued to read for a few seconds more, before it finally dawned on me. Slowly, I lowered the comic and looked towards the end of my bed.

Sitting there, reading a *Captain Bin-Man* comic with his dragon-like claws, was the dragon toy from the beansprout box.

YOUR LIFE IS ABOUT TO CHANGE

Two things were clear to me:

The toy dragon was not a toy.

Whoever makes Panda Cottage's fortune cookies had really raised their game this time.

CHAPTER 2
BOY MEETS DRAGON

Quiz:

There's a dragon sitting on your bed, reading your comics. Do you:

a) Let him finish reading

b) Politely introduce yourself

c) Ignore him and hope he goes away

d) Poke him with a rolled-up comic

"Ouch! What did you do that for?"

I went with option D.

"Sorry," I said. "Are you … real?"

"Of course I'm real," said the creature, with a look of mild irritation. "So stop poking me."

"But you … you're a…" I couldn't believe what I was about to say. "You're a dragon." Even as the words left my mouth I couldn't grasp what was happening. I was definitely never eating beansprouts again.

"No, I'm not," he replied, which caught me off guard. I mean, sure, I had got it wrong about him being a toy, but I was pretty sure I was spot on about this.

"What do you mean, you're not?" I said. "You obviously are. I mean … look at you!"

"Dragons are about twelve metres long," he said. "Some of them can be twice that, in fact. Do I look that big to you?"

He definitely didn't. He was no longer

than a ruler. The kind of ruler that fits in your pencil case.

"So, what are you, then?" I asked.

"I'm a Mini-Dragon," he said, puffing out his chest and looking very pleased with himself.

"But … you *are* a dragon?" I said. "Just a really small one."

"Oh no," he said, shaking his little head. "Small dragons are much bigger. I'm a *Mini-*Dragon. Basically it goes: Large Dragon, Regular Dragon, Small Dragon, Komodo Dragon, Little Dragon, Tiny Dragon, Snap Dragon, Mini-Dragon.

"Mini-Dragons might be the littlest of the dragons," he continued. "But we're also the best."

"In what way?" I asked.

"Well, we can do everything that the others can do, apart from Snap Dragons, and most dragons are starting to think they aren't real dragons anyway. Plus we can talk. Don't know if you noticed?"

"Now that you mention it…"

"And unlike other dragons, there's hardly any chance of us accidentally squashing you."

"Hardly?" I asked.

"Well, there *was* this one time with an uncle of mine who was very overweight," said the Mini-Dragon. "But my family doesn't like to talk about that…"

"So you can fly?" I asked.

"Piece of cake," he said. "Watch, I'll show you."

I looked around my room. "In here? I don't think that's a good idea."

"Don't worry, I know what I'm doing," he said, before sprinting towards the end of my bed, jumping off and… Well, it all got a bit complicated after that.

It wasn't exactly flying. But it wasn't exactly not-flying, either. It reminded me of skimming stones at the beach – though a lot less graceful. The Mini-Dragon crashed into the wall

and then
    my wardrobe
and then my desk

and then my window

and then my bed again
and then a shelf

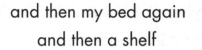

and then the ceiling
and then my chest of drawers
        and then another wall
and then two more shelves
        and then me

        and then finally
        the floor...

It was certainly flying-*esque* but really it was more a kind of delayed falling.

"Guess I'm a bit rusty..." he said, dusting himself off and looking flustered.

I stared around the remains of my room. Clothes and comics were scattered everywhere. Books and toys that had been neatly arranged on shelves now lay all over the floor.

"Have you ever actually flown before?" I asked suspiciously.

The Mini-Dragon stroked his chin. "That depends on what you mean by 'before'..."

"Like ... ever?"

"Oh. No. But I think I'm close to getting the hang of it... Hey, what's that banging noise?"

That banging noise was the sound of Mum stomping her way up the stairs.

"Quick, hide," I said, opening my sock drawer and chucking him in.

Suddenly the door swung open and there was Mum. Her head turned slowly, scanning the room. I watched her eyes bulge and her face redden. If she were a normal mum, this would be the point where she exploded.

But instead she closed her eyes, put her palms together and raised her left leg so that she was balancing on her right. She took a couple of deep, long breaths as the red in her face drained away.

"Kindly explain yourself," she said, in an eerily calm voice.

"Um … I don't suppose you'd believe a dragon did it?" I asked, giving her my best "sorry" smile.

"*Mini*-Dragon," said a muffled voice from the sock drawer. Luckily, Mum didn't seem to hear.

Unsurprisingly, she didn't buy the dragon story.

"We talked about this, Eric," said Mum. "You're now officially on **STRIKE ONE**."

"But Mum—"

"No buts," said Mum firmly, still balancing on one leg. "I think an early night is in order, too."

I looked at my watch. "It's only half seven!"

"You should have thought of that before you decided to demolish your room. Good night, Eric." Mum came out of her yoga pose and left the room.

"Sorry about that," said the Mini-Dragon, popping his head out as I opened the drawer.

I could tell from his awkward smile and the embarrassed look on his face that he meant it, but it didn't change the fact that I'd got a strike.

"What's 'Strike One'?" asked the Mini-Dragon.

Even thinking about it made me anxious, but I told him anyway. "It's my birthday soon and I've asked for the fastest electric scooter on the market – a Thunderbolt. I've wanted one for ages. My best friend Jayden has one and he swears that going downhill with the wind behind you, you can break the sound barrier.

Not sure if that's one hundred per cent true, but I really want to find out. Mum and Dad said that I can get one as long as I don't get three strikes between now and my birthday. Well, that's me on one."

The Mini-Dragon nodded sympathetically. "Even though I'm pretty sure I'm close to mastering it, I'll try to avoid flying indoors again."

"Thanks," I said.

"So, your birthday, huh?" he said. "How old will you be?"

"Nine," I said.

The Mini-Dragon nodded. "Ah, nine. A good age. I should know, I'm nine right now. In dragon years, anyway."

"What's that in human years?" I asked.

"Nine," he said. "Yeah, years are the same length for dragons. Except we follow the Dragonian Calendar where every four years, instead of giving February the extra day, we stick it in between 25th and 26th December and make Christmas twice as long."

I thought about this for a few moments. "Wow," I said. "That's a much better idea."

"I know, right?"

"ERIC, THAT BETTER NOT BE YOU ON THE PHONE TO JAYDEN! GET TO BED!" shouted Mum.

"I'm not," I shouted back. "On the phone, I mean. I'm just getting into bed."

"I suppose I should go to sleep before I get another strike," I said, lowering my voice.

"I could do with some sleep myself," said the Mini-Dragon. "It's been quite an eventful day."

"I'm not exactly set up for Mini-Dragons," I said, looking around for a suitable bed.

The chair at my desk was comfy to sit on, but probably not to sleep on... Or maybe I could make some kind of nest from all the scattered comics on my floor... Or...

"I'm fine here," he said, nestling down in the sock drawer. "Much comfier than a box of beansprouts, that's for sure."

"All right, then," I said. "Well, goodnight... Wait – what's your name?"

"Pan," he replied. "Pan Long."

I might have made a joke about his surname and him being so short, but I decided against it for two reasons:

1. I'm sure he had heard them all.

2. If you have the surname Crisp, you don't joke about other people's surnames.

"Nice to meet you Pan. I'm Eric." I held out my hand and shook one of his little claws.

"Nice to meet you, too, Eric."

As I lay on my bed, I couldn't stop

thinking about that night's events. I mean, there couldn't *really* be a Mini-Dragon sleeping in my sock drawer at that very moment, right? One that could talk? And fly slightly better than a rock? Was I coming down with something? Was it all just a weird dream? Was he some kind of scaly hallucination?

I placed my hands over my ears.

Hallucinations didn't usually snore as loudly as this one though, did they?

The next morning confirmed Pan was definitely real. It took all day to clean my room, mainly because Pan insisted on reading every comic he came across before putting it back. At least it gave me plenty of time to ask him questions.

"Where are you from?" I said, putting a bunch of action figures back up on my shelf.

"China," he replied. "I lived in a cave with my parents. There were mountains everywhere, it was great. Plenty of room for a young Mini-Dragon to learn to fly. It's these walls you see, that's the problem. No room."

"Yeah, must be the walls," I said, laughing. "So if it was so great, why did you wind up here, then?"

"Humans," said Pan, suddenly sounding

sad. "They knocked down our cave to build their huge buildings. My parents were OK, they could fly to safety in the mountains, but me... Well, you've seen my flying. I'll admit there's still a bit of work to do there. Normally Mini-Dragons don't leave home until they turn ten, but Mum and Dad thought it best that I went to live with relatives. So they managed to smuggle me into a box of beansprouts and that's how I ended up here in Mexico."

There was an awkward silence as I stared at Pan.

"Did you say Mexico?"

Pan nodded. "You know, it's not as hot as I thought it would be."

"Um... I think you'd better take a look at this," I said, picking up the globe that Pan had knocked over the night before. "This is Mexico," I said, pointing to North America.

Then I spun the globe around.

"And this is where you are," I said.

"England."

Pan stared at the spot beneath my finger, scratching his head. "Hmm. I was starting to wonder when Auntie Maria and Uncle Fernando were going to show up.

What am I going to do now?"

"I guess you can stay with me," I said hesitantly. "For a bit, I mean. Until we figure things out."

"Wow, thank you," said Pan, throwing his tiny arms around my wrist.

"Er, you're welcome," I said, patting him awkwardly on the head. "Wait a minute, though, if you're from China, how come you can speak perfect English?"

"Picked it up on the boat over," said Pan matter-of-factly. "The crew watched a lot of English TV and Mini-Dragons are extremely fast learners."

Except when it comes to flying, I thought.

It was nearly time for dinner when Pan had finished reading the last comic, making the tidying mission officially complete.

I was just about to congratulate Pan on a job well done when I heard a terrible sound.

DIIIIIIING-DONGGGGGG!

DIIIIIIING-DONGGGGGG!

"Oh no," I groaned.

"What's a ding-dong?" asked Pan.

"That's the doorbell," I said, closing my
eyes. "And at this time on a Saturday it
means only one thing: Toby."

CHAPTER 3
GAMES NIGHT

"Come on, Crispo," a voice shouted through the letter box. "Let me in, I'm starving. And the longer I'm out here, the less time there is for me to whoop you at *Total Combat*."

"Who's that?" asked Pan, pressing his tiny head against the window.

"That's Toby from next door," I said. "Tonight's games night."

"Ooh, games night! That sounds fun," said Pan, with a gleam in his eye.

Games night is *not* fun. Games night is the opposite of fun. If you were to rank all the things to do in the entire universe in order of fun, this would be the end of that list:

49,509. Fighting a shark

49,510. Going to the dentist

49,511. Being a dentist

49,512. Being your own dentist

49,513. Fighting a shark that's brought his mates along for backup

49,514. Fighting a dentist shark

49,515. Going to the opera

49,516. Fighting a dentist shark that's brought his mates along for backup. At the opera

49,517. Ranking all the things to do in the entire universe in order of fun

49,518. Games night

And yes, there are exactly 49,518 things to do in the entire universe. I know because I once got so bored during games night that I counted them all.

My mum came up with games night after one of her yoga meditations. She felt sorry for our next-door neighbour Toby, who was always being left at home by his parents, who both have **Mega-Important** jobs in The City (wherever that is).

The one thing to know about Toby is that he always gets what he wants.

All the latest toys? Yep.

A 97-inch television in his bedroom? Of course.

His own credit card? He's got five.

Sure, I hear you say, but is he *happy*?

Yes. Yes, he is. The best thing I can say about Toby is that he doesn't go to the same school as me. He goes to the poshest, most expensive school in town. I've only ever seen it in brochures, but all the kids look just like Toby. Even some of the girls. Going there would be my worst nightmare.

"Can I come?" asked Pan.

I gave Pan a glance that said "Of course not, you're a dragon!", but he didn't seem to understand, so I said, "Of course not, you're a dragon!"

Pan looked dejected.

"Don't be like that," I said. "Trust me, Toby is the last person in the world you want to meet. Maybe once he's gone we can play something, but until then, if you can just stay here... Please?"

"All right," said Pan. "I'm sure I'll find something to do."

I began to close the door when a thought occurred to me. "And Pan?"

"Yeah, yeah," he said. "No flying!"

"Thanks. I'll try and smuggle some food up for you later."

"Oh, that's OK," said Pan. "I'm not hungry."

I closed the door and wondered to myself, *what does a Mini-Dragon even eat*?

I knew exactly what a *Toby* ate: anything put in front of him. Toby had almost finished his dinner by the time I got downstairs. Mum and Dad were staring at him, fascinated, as if they were watching a nature documentary.

"Oh, here he is – finally!" said Toby, spaghetti strands dripping from his mouth.

How to describe what Toby looks like? Mum says it's rude to use the word "fat". She prefers the word "robust". Toby is massively robust.

"Your mum let me in, by the way. Probably would have died from hunger if I'd had to wait for you."

"Yeah, close one that..." Dad mumbled.

Mum put a plate of spaghetti down in front of me. She leaned in and, glancing sideways at Toby, whispered in my ear, "He's on his third helping. Any longer and I'm not sure I would have been able to keep it for you."

I smiled and tucked in. Toby and I didn't agree on much, but Mum's spaghetti being awesome was definitely one of the few things on the list.

"So, Toby, will you be coming to Eric's party next Saturday?" asked Mum.

Please say no, please say no, please say no.

"Thought I might swing by," said Toby. "Help liven things up. You still getting that new Thunderbolt, Eric?"

"As long as he keeps out of trouble," said Dad.

"Yeah, Mum bought me one of those last month," yawned Toby. "But I said 'One? What if that breaks? Then I'd have none.' She saw sense and bought me another two just to be safe. Haven't actually used any of them yet, though."

I noticed my mum frowning. "Well, Eric

will definitely only be getting *one*. And that's only if—"

"I keep out of trouble," I finished for her.

"All right," said Toby, shoving his plate aside. "Time for Eric's weekly humiliation at *Total Combat*."

"Can I finish my dinner first?" I asked.

Toby rolled his eyes as if I was the one being unreasonable, but reluctantly nodded.

I was just wrapping the last strands of spaghetti around my fork when I saw it.

A small scaly figure strolled casually past the kitchen door.

I wolfed down the last forkful then bolted out of my chair just in time to see Pan's tail disappearing into the sitting room.

"Wow, someone's in a hurry to lose tonight," said Toby. "Hey, what's that?"

He was pointing at Pan.

I froze.

Funnily enough, so did Pan. He looked like a little dragon figurine as he sat on the end of the couch, facing the television.

"Umm ... a toy?" I said.

"When did you get it?" he asked, looking at me suspiciously. Toby made it his business to know about every toy I had, so that he could get the same one or, preferably, something even better.

"Actually, it's Posy's," I fibbed.

Toby didn't look convinced. "Hardly seems like a toy for a two year old."

"It's the only toy she has that she doesn't eat," I said.

Toby considered this for a second then nodded. "Yeah, I guess that makes sense. Ugly little thing though, isn't it? I prefer my dragons massive and with rocket launchers."

Pan remained still but I noticed that his expression had turned sour.

"Maybe he'll bring you luck," laughed Toby, picking up his controller. "After last week, you could use it."

As long as Pan kept up the charade, I didn't see the harm in him watching us play, so I grabbed my controller and sat down.

As I mentioned before: games night is not fun. You might think because it involves video games it would be, but you'd be wrong. Playing against Toby is a chore. You don't play to win, you play to lose. Otherwise you risk a repeat of last year's infamous *Soccer Stars* Boxing Day incident where Toby went nuclear after I beat him 5–0. Even my dad considers it the worst football-related meltdown he's ever seen.

I've actually become quite good at making it look like I'm trying to win. It's not just a case of pressing random buttons, you have to throw in a few special moves, block a few attacks, sell it like you care.

After building up an eight-game losing streak, though, my mind had started to wander to thoughts of how Pan could have ended up on my couch watching me get digitally beaten up when he was supposed to be in Mexico.

And then I saw that he wasn't watching. Pan had vanished. Just as confusingly, I was no longer losing at the game. Not even close. I was destroying Toby. And I had no idea how, until I looked down and saw Pan in my lap, furiously tap-dancing across the buttons.

Even though the score was still only 8–1, Toby went ballistic. He didn't even notice Pan as he stormed out of the door screaming, **"MRS CRISP! MRS CRISP! ERIC'S CHEATING AGAIN!"**

I looked down. Pan grinned back at me. "Did I mention," he said, "that Mini-Dragons are *excellent* at video games?"

CHAPTER 4

WEEKEND WEEDING

Thankfully Mum hadn't really believed
Toby when he told her that I had cheated
and, since he couldn't prove it, the
matter had been dropped. So I hadn't
got a second strike, which was good.
Unfortunately the universe decided to
punish me anyway, when the next day
Mum announced that the back garden
needed weeding before my birthday
party next weekend. And guess who was
nominated to do it?

Bingo.

So that's why I was spending my Sunday trying to pull the toughest weed in the entire world out of the ground.

"This is boring," said Pan, who had sneaked outside to stretch his tail for a bit. He was sitting on an upturned plant pot, kicking his little legs aimlessly off the side. "Want to play video games instead? Or read comics? Or, well, anything that isn't this?"

"I'm not doing this because I enjoy it," I said. "I'm doing it because if I don't then my birthday party next Saturday won't be happening. At least, that's what Mum says. She might be bluffing, but it's not worth the risk."

"Ooh, I love parties," said Pan. "We had one for my last birthday, it was so much fun. We played all kinds of things, like *Pass the Boulder*, *What's that Rock?*, *Pin the Tail on the Dragon*, *Musical Stones*, *Duck Duck Dragon* and *Hot-Scotch*. Will you be playing those games?"

"Probably not those *exact* games, no," I said.

"Can I come?" he asked.

I hesitated. "I'm not sure that's a good idea, Pan."

"Why not?" he asked, looking a bit hurt.

"Well ... this might come as a surprise to you, but most people think dragons don't exist."

Pan looked shocked. "Even Mini-Dragons?"

I nodded. "Especially Mini-Dragons. They'd be ... frightened."

Pan gave this some thought then said, "Well, I suppose I *can* look quite intimidating."

"Exactly," I said. The truth was that I had watched enough movies to know that any time an alien or a magical creature makes friends with a kid, there's always someone who tries to kidnap it for their mad experiments. I didn't want to alarm Pan over this, but I thought it best if the number of people who knew about him was kept at one.

But there might be another way.

"What if you do that thing where you freeze," I said. "Maybe I could keep you close by at the party and pretend you're a toy or something."

Pan perked up a little at this. "That could work. Although I'll have to practise at controlling it – it usually only happens when I'm scared— I mean, IN DANGER! It only happens when I'm in danger."

"So that's why you froze when Toby was around, and when you first met me?" I said.

"Mini-Dragons are excellent at detecting threats," he said. "And I quickly realized you're not one. Toby, on the other hand..."

"You know, it might not be a good idea

for you to be out here," I said. "Someone might see you."

Pan looked up at our massive garden fence. "I think I'll be OK. And I checked, your parents are inside—"

"Eric!" shouted Mum.

My heart almost popped out of my chest. Instinctively, I grabbed Pan and shoved him under an empty plant pot.

"Jayden's here," said Mum.

"Who's Jayden?" asked the plant pot.

"My best friend," I whispered.

"Hey, Eric," said Jayden, pushing his sunglasses back. Jayden almost always wore shorts and T-shirts, even when it wasn't ideal – like in winter. But they were perfect clothes for gardening.

Jayden looked at me with suspicion. "Why are you smiling at me like that?" he asked.

"Can't believe you roped me into this," grumbled Jayden. "Look at my hands, they're gross." I sprang back as he tried to prove his point by rubbing them in my hair.

"Get off," I laughed.

"Still, a job well done, I'd say," said Jayden, admiring a tiny patch of soil.

"Um ... you know we're not finished, right?" I said, motioning towards the huge area of garden still to do.

Jayden was stunned. "But we've been at this for hours!"

"It's been *fifteen minutes*."

Jayden let out a huge sigh and

reluctantly reached for his trowel.

Even with Jayden helping, things didn't seem to be getting done much more quickly, but at least it wasn't as boring. We had a good laugh about Toby trying to get me in trouble. I left out the part about the Mini-Dragon.

Jayden shook his head. "I've said it before, but I'll say it again – that boy's a nightmare. Hey, where do you want this?"

I let out a gasp. Jayden had picked up the plant pot with Pan inside it.

As he pointed it towards me, I could see Pan looking alarmed, his arms and legs pressed up against the side, to stop him from falling out.

"What?" asked Jayden, noticing my expression.

"Er ... that's where it goes!" I blurted out, pointing to where it had just been.

"OK," said Jayden. "Odd place to leave
it, if you ask me, but whatever."

Jayden put the plant pot back and I
breathed a huge sigh of relief.

I also felt guilty for not telling him about
Pan. He is my best friend after all. I wanted

to, but I wasn't sure if it was a good idea or not. I would have to give it some thought.

Mum made us some sandwiches for lunch and, after we'd finished, Jayden hurried home before I made him garden again. Feeling guilty about how long he had been hiding, I brought out a sandwich for Pan. When I lifted the plant pot I found him curled up at the bottom of it, asleep. I had to admit, he looked pretty cute.

Then he belched.

"Excuse me!" he said, rubbing his eyes.

"You can come out now," I said. "Jayden's gone. Here, I brought you this – thought you might be hungry."

Pan shook his head. "No, thank you, I'm fine," he said. "So Jayden, he's your friend. Like Toby?"

I burst out laughing. "No, not like Toby," I said. "A friend is someone you actually *enjoy* spending time with."

"Ah…" said Pan. "Like me and you."

"Um, yeah, I guess," I said, feeling a little embarrassed.

"You guys laughed a lot," noted Pan.

"Jayden's pretty funny," I said.

"Mini-Dragons are funny, too. Here, pull on this," said Pan, holding out a claw. Without thinking I gave it a tug, at which point Pan let out a massive fart. At the same time a blast of fire left Pan's mouth, lighting up the fart in a small but awesome ball of flame.

I looked at Pan. Pan looked at me. Then we fell on to the grass laughing. "That was pretty funny, I'll give you that," I said, wiping a tear from my eye. "And your fire-breathing is definitely better than your flying."

I was about to request a repeat performance when I froze, like a Mini-Dragon sensing danger.

There, standing in my garden, his jaw on the ground, was Toby.

CHAPTER 5

AN OFFER HE CAN REFUSE

I stood there, staring at Toby. What had he seen? What had he heard? I hadn't decided yet whether Jayden knowing about Pan was a good idea, but I had no doubt that Toby knowing was definitely bad.

"I should have guessed!" said Toby, folding his arms.

"Toby, I can explain!" I said. I looked around at Pan, who was in frozen mode, not that it would do us any good now.

"Don't waste your breath, Crispo," he said, puffing out his chest. "I should have known that it wasn't your sister's dragon."

"Toby, listen—"

"You just didn't want *me* playing with your cool new toy," he said.

I opened my mouth to reply, then paused. Did Toby still think Pan was a toy?

"You're so selfish, Crispo. After all I do for you. I always let you look at my new stuff!"

Wow, he really *did* think Pan was a toy.

"I heard some muttering just before I came in," said Toby. "So it talks, huh? That's not so impressive, but the fire-breathing thing – even I have to admit, I've never seen that in an action toy before. Well, it looks like today's your lucky day, Crispo!"

"Why's that?" I said suspiciously, realizing at last that Toby had only caught the tail end of the fart.

"I'm going to buy him off you," said Toby.

"You're going to do *what*?" I said.

"How does ten pounds sound?" said Toby, taking his wallet out of his pocket.

"No."

"All right, fine – twenty," said Toby.

"No," I repeated as I picked up Pan and my trowel.

Toby began to thumb through the notes in his wallet. "Playing hardball, eh? I like it. I'll go up to fifty."

"Go away, Toby," I said, returning to the weeding, with Pan right next to me just to be safe.

Toby was starting to get annoyed. "One hundred pounds – my final offer!"

It was a lot of money, and I had no doubt Toby could afford it, but I didn't hesitate even for a second. "Toby, I wouldn't sell him to you for all the money in the world."

"Fine, then," said Toby, storming off. "I'll just go and find one on the internet. There's probably a better version anyway."

"Wow, he's really not that bright, is he?" said Pan once Toby was out of sight.

"He's really not," I agreed.

"Oh well. Can we do something fun now?" asked Pan.

"I still have to finish the weeding," I said.

Pan held a claw to his brow and began to survey the garden, like a general looking out over a battlefield. Except the enemy was the weeds, and they were everywhere. "All right, let me try something," he said.

"Huh?"

Pan dived into the soil and began furiously slicing up the weeds with his claws, like a mini-chainsaw. In less than a minute there wasn't a single weed still in the ground.

My jaw was hanging open. "Wow."

"Turns out Mini-Dragons are *excellent* at weeding," said Pan.

"Thanks, Pan," I said, trying not to think about the time we could have saved if he'd just tried that a couple of hours ago.

"Thanks for not selling me," said Pan when we got back to my room.

"No problem," I said. "We're friends, Pan. Friends don't sell friends."

For such a small dragon, the smile on Pan's face was pretty big. "Friends like Jayden?" he said. "Not Toby?"

"Like Jayden," I said. "Definitely not like Toby."

Remembering I still had the sandwich from earlier, I offered it to Pan again. Once more he declined.

"But you must be starving," I said. "You haven't eaten since you got here. What did you eat back in China?"

"Oh, lots of things," said Pan, a dreamy look in his eyes. "I had a very varied diet. Let's see, there was roasted mountain goat, fried mountain goat, barbecued mountain goat, grilled mountain goat and smoked mountain goat."

"So, mostly mountain goat, then?" I asked.

"Mostly, yeah," said Pan.

"I'm afraid we're a bit short on those around here," I said.

"No worries," said Pan. "Besides, I've eaten plenty since I arrived. I found tons to eat in your food basket."

"Food basket?" I said, scratching my head. "What food basket?"

"That one over there in the corner."

My stomach dropped.

"You mean my clothes basket," I said. "Where I put my dirty washing?"

I opened the basket and took out my school clothes. Or what was left of them. They were ruined – with hundreds of tiny holes.

Horrified, I turned to Pan.

"I thought they went in there because you were finished with them," he said. "That's why I didn't eat any of your socks. Well, that and because it's rude to eat your bed."

I sat down on my bed, closed my eyes and took a long, deep breath. I hate to admit it but as I sat there, for a split second I did wonder if it was too late to take Toby's money.

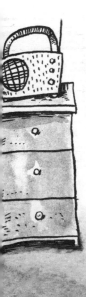

CHAPTER 6
RETURNING THE DRAGON

"Sorry Eric's late, Miss Biggs," said Mum the following day as I took my seat in class. "Emergency shopping trip. There was a ... *situation* at home with his school uniform. Moths apparently. Big ones." Mum looked at me suspiciously as she said this. Moths had been the only excuse I could think of. It was far fetched but, not as far fetched as what had actually happened.

Needless to say, this was **STRIKE TWO**.

I did try to argue that since it was moths, it was unfair to blame me, but then Mum pointed out that I must have left my window open to let them in.

My teacher's eyes were fixed on Mum. There was a sharp intake of breath from the whole class. Miss Biggs lived up to her name. Comparisons were often made to abominable snowwomen, owing to her size, general evil demeanour and her massive white perm. Unlike the yeti, though, Miss Biggs definitely existed.

Jayden, sitting at the table to my right, leaned over and whispered, "Dude, she's giving your mum the Biggs Death Stare!"

Miss Biggs's infamous Death Stare was the stuff of legend. It was so powerful that kids would confess to things they hadn't done just to get her to stop. It was like she could look right into your soul and then give it a vicious karate chop. And it worked just as well on adults. Beads of sweat were already forming on Mum's forehead.

"Er, yes, well… See you at home, Eric!" shouted Mum as she dashed out of the door.

Miss Biggs redirected her stare towards me. On any other day, I would probably already be confessing to letting off the stink bomb during lunch last Thursday (even though I didn't).

But today, I barely paid her any attention.

I was too busy worrying about how Pan was getting on. And then, as I saw Mum's car drive off out of the window, my mind turned to Pan's parents, who were probably wondering the same thing.

"I've had a terrible day," said Pan when I got home.

"What happened?" I asked.

"Well, first I decided to go exploring ... then I ran into Pusskin ... then I ran *from* Pusskin ... but I managed to give her the slip by hiding out in Posy's room... Posy invited me to dinner ... but it turned out I was the main course!"

Pan held up his tail. The bite mark was still there. "Luckily I made it back to your room," he said. "And I haven't left since."

"Sorry, Pan," I said. "This probably
wasn't what your parents had in mind when
they sent you away."

"Probably not," agreed Pan.

"I was thinking about that today at school," I said. "We need to find out how you ended up here and not in Mexico. And, if we can, find another way to get you there."

Pan looked confused. "You ... don't want me here?"

"No, no," I said, shaking my head. "It's not that at all. I'd love you to stay ... it's just that your parents sent you to be with your aunt and uncle ... and now you're here. They'll be worried. They sent you to be safe and to be looked after by other dragons and now you're stuck here with me, sleeping in a sock drawer, eating dirty clothes and being chased by cats and eaten by toddlers."

"It was just one cat and one toddler," said Pan quietly.

"I just don't think they'd be very happy," I said. "I don't want you to go, at least not so soon, but I think it's the right thing to do."

Pan still didn't look convinced. "So, how do we find out what happened?" he asked.

"We need to go back to where you came from," I said.

"China?"

"Er ... no, after that."

"What do you mean, where do my beansprouts come from?" asked Mr Song, as he laid out chopsticks in preparation for a busy evening at Panda Cottage. He looked at me suspiciously. "You're not from the Department of Health, are you?"

"I'm eight years old," I said.

"You didn't answer my question," said Mr Song.

I sighed. "No, Mr Song, I'm not from the the Department of Health."

"Good," he said. "Panda Cottage is the most hygienic Chinese restaurant in town!"

I was about to remind him that it was the *only* Chinese restaurant in town, but decided against it. "Yeah, I know that, it's uh … for a school project."

"Hmm. All right, then," said Mr Song, looking slightly less suspicious. "They come directly from China. I have good connections there. Best ingredients. Best prices."

I had guessed that much, but it didn't explain why Pan had ended up here and not Mexico.

"Although…" said Mr Song. "Our latest shipment technically comes from Mexico. Quite annoying, really."

"Mexico?" I said, perking up.

"Yes… My pal Dave had a Panda Cottage franchise out in Mexico City. He thought he could make a fortune selling Chinese food to the Mexican wrestlers. It was a good plan, except for one thing – he's a lousy cook. He couldn't follow the recipes and ended up making all the wrestlers sick. He had to flee the city from dozens of angry *Luchadores* – that's Spanish for wrestler – and return to England. And, of course, all this happens on the day he was due to get a huge stock delivery. No one's there to sign for it, so they just stick it on another boat and send it all to me. So now I'm out of pocket and I've got beansprouts coming out of my ears. Do you want any? Here, take a box. Take a dozen!"

"No, thank you," I said as he tried to force boxes into my arms. "I don't suppose your friend is planning on going back to Mexico any time soon?"

Mr Song frowned. "No, but I did just find out today that he's about to open a new restaurant. In *Antarctica*."

I raised my eyebrows.

"Please, don't get me started," sighed Mr Song.

"Well, that was a waste of time," said Pan, who had been hiding in my backpack, as we left Panda Cottage.

"Yeah, unless you fancy living in Antarctica," I said.

"Not really."

"Then I think we're stuck with each other," I said. I felt an odd sensation and realized after a moment that it was relief.

"That's all right," said Pan. "My aunt and uncle aren't that nice, to be honest. They came to stay with us once. They were always criticizing me, telling my parents I needed to be toughened up. I'm not sure I would have been very happy living with them."

"Hey, Eric, wait up!" Min Song bounded towards me.

"Oh, hi, Min," I said, trying to sound like there definitely wasn't a tiny dragon in my bag.

Min frowned. "What are you up to?"

"What do you mean?" I asked innocently.

"I don't know, you've been acting well strange today," she said. "First you show up late to class, then you spend the rest of the day staring into space. Then I overhear you talking to my dad about beansprouts for a school project that I know you don't have. And now I've just seen you talking to yourself. Are you all right, Eric?"

"I'm fine," I said.

Min didn't look convinced, but maybe she would have dropped it if what happened next hadn't happened.

"*Attishoooo!*" sneezed my backpack.

Min and I stared at each other for what seemed like forever. For a second I considered pretending to have a cold, but the look on Min's face made it clear I wasn't going to be able to lie my way out of this one. I thought about running, but Min was the fastest girl in school.

"Hurry up and open the bag," said Min, looking at her watch. "I haven't got all day."

Reluctantly, I unzipped my backpack. Pan popped his head out. He gave her a little wave.

Min let out a massive scream then sprinted back up the road.

Me and Pan stood there in stunned silence. "Well, that seemed to go well," said Pan.

CHAPTER 7

MINI-DRAGONS: THE FACTS

I chased after Min all the way back to Panda Cottage then lost sight of her. With guests starting to arrive, Min's dad was a lot less accommodating.

"Sorry, kid," he said, "now's not a good time. And if it's Min you're after, you'll have to wait to see her at school. Now, are you sure you won't take a couple of dozen boxes of beansprouts?"

"No, thank you," I said, before giving up and going home.

I barely slept at all that night, terrified that

Min would alert the authorities. With every squeak of the stairs, I expected a bunch of men in dark suits and sunglasses to burst through my door and take Pan.

But they never did.

The following day at school I tried to speak to Min, but she kept avoiding me. In class, she had swapped chairs so that she was at the other end of the room. At break, I waited for her in the corridor. As soon as she saw me, she spun on her heels and marched off in the opposite direction, disappearing into the girls' toilets.

At lunch I saw her sitting at a table and was just about to finally get near her, when Jayden, who was sitting at the next table, shouted, "Hey, Eric, I saved a seat for you."

A startled-looking Min glanced up at me, before quickly grabbing her tray and rushing off.

"What was all that about?" asked Jayden as I sat down.

"Nothing," I said.

"Hey, want to come round mine tonight?" he asked. "It's been *ages* since we hung out."

"We hung out on Sunday," I said.

"I mean hang out and do something *fun*," said Jayden.

"Not tonight, sorry," I said.

As much as I wanted to hang out with Jayden, I needed to get hold of Min and convince her not to tell anyone.

"Tomorrow, then?" he suggested.

"No, I can't do then, either," I said. "Toby comes over on Wednesdays."

Jayden sighed. "Thursday?"

Meeting up with Jayden meant leaving Pan alone, and I already felt bad enough about him having to hide out from Pusskin in my room all day. On the other hand, Jayden was my best friend and I had to make time for him, too. ARRRGHHH! Things would be much simpler if I could just tell Jayden the truth. But given how badly Min had reacted, that didn't seem like a great idea.

"Fine, it doesn't matter," said Jayden, as I realized I had been too busy thinking all this over to answer his question.

"Yeah – Thursday," I blurted out. "Thursday's fine."

When had my life got so complicated?

Min continued to avoid me for the rest of the afternoon and the whole of the next day, too. On the up side, Pan still hadn't been dragon-napped.

We had spent some time trying to find things Pan could eat that weren't also things I needed to wear. So far he had sampled the following food items and found them disgusting:

Leftover spaghetti

Cold pizza

Fruit

Biscuits

Crisps

Beans on toast

Cornflakes

Cheese sandwiches

Ham sandwiches

Tomato ketchup sandwiches

I was especially surprised that he didn't care for the ketchup sandwiches – that's my signature dish! It's taken me years to perfect the recipe (two bits of bread, half a bottle of ketchup). Honestly, there's no accounting for taste with some Mini-Dragons.

The next evening I was so busy worrying about Min, and Pan's diet, that I barely put any effort into losing to Toby. In fact I was so distracted that when Toby left to go to the toilet, I didn't notice until about five minutes later that he hadn't come back.

I rushed up the stairs to find him in my room, going through my things.

"What are you up to, Toby?" I said.

"Nothing!" he said, trying to look innocent, which was quite difficult given that he was holding my pants in his hands.

I glared at him.

"All right, fine," he said, tossing my pants away. "I couldn't find that stupid dragon anywhere online."

"So you were planning on stealing mine?"

"I offered to pay you! Still will, in fact. Come on, Eric, let's make a deal."

I glared at Toby. "The only deal I'm going to make with you, is that if you go home right now, I won't tell Mum you were raking through my underwear."

Toby glared right back at me. "Fine," he said, "but that dragon *will* be mine. I always get what I want."

"Not this time," I said.

"We'll see, Crispo," he said, before slamming my bedroom door behind him.

"Pan?" I said, looking round the room.

"A little help," came a muffled voice.

I opened the drawer immediately below the one Toby had been going through. Inside, a pair of socks rocked back and forth. I reached in and pulled out Pan.

"Thanks," he said. "It was the only place I could think to hide. But socks are much easier to get into than out of."

Toby had come closer than he would ever know to getting his hands on Pan. *Great*, I thought. *Another thing to worry about.*

I didn't even bother trying to speak to Min on Thursday. I knew she wouldn't want to talk to me, but at least she hadn't blabbed to anyone.

Then, after school, something unexpected happened. I was just leaving the house to go and meet Jayden at the park and there she was, standing on my doorstep, holding a brown paper bag under one arm and an enormous book under the other.

"Can we talk?" she asked.

"Er ... sure."

We went upstairs to my room.

"You're back early," said Pan, looking up at us from behind a *Slug Man* comic.

"You're supposed to freeze," I said.

Pan shook his head. "Nah, she's not a threat. Are you?"

"I don't think so," said Min. She turned to me. "Sorry about the other day. It was just a bit of a shock, you know, seeing a Mini-Dragon for the first time."

"Tell me about it," I said. "Wait, how do you know he's a Mini-Dragon?"

A smile formed on Min's face. "I've been doing some research."

She slammed the huge book on to my bed.

"Wow," I said. "That's a *big* book."

"All books look big to me," said Pan.

"I found it in our attic," said Min. "It's been in our family for generations. It's one of the oldest Chinese books in existence, containing untold secrets—"

"Wait a minute," I said. "Why does it have a barcode on the back? And it's written in English…"

"It's uh … mystical…"

"It still has a 'Buy One Get One Free' sticker on the front," I said, pointing.

"Fine, then," Min said, folding her arms. "We got it a few years ago from the bargain bookshop on the high street. But I'm telling you, it has everything, even a section about Mini-Dragons. That's how I knew what he was."

"His name's Pan," I said, flipping through the book.

"Nice to meet you, Pan," Min said. "I don't know why I was so scared of you, you're actually quite handsome up close."

"I like her already," beamed Pan, puffing out his tiny chest.

"Here's the bit about Mini-Dragons," I said.

Mini-Dragons

Often mistaken for baby dragons or dragons that are very far away, Mini-Dragons are similar in almost every way to regular dragons, except for several key differences:

1. They can talk.
2. The average size of a Mini-Dragon is 15cm – about the size of a spring roll.
3. They are quick learners – often able to pick up new skills with very little effort. Unfortunately, this can lead to them becoming overconfident in their abilities, sometimes with disastrous consequences.
4. Of all the dragons, they are easily the most stubborn.

"No, we're not!" protested Pan.

"There's also a bit about what they eat," said Min as I turned the page.

"*Mini-Dragons: What they eat and what they do not eat,*" I said.

"Title's a bit of a mouthful," grinned Pan.

Mini-Dragons' main food source is the mountain goat. Due to their relative sizes, one mountain goat can provide enough food to feed a family of four Mini-Dragons for an entire month.

Other than goat, Mini-Dragons have shown throughout the years a fondness for human clothing and prawn crackers.

"What's a prawn cracker?" asked Pan.

"I thought you might ask that," said Min, handing him the brown paper bag. From it Pan took out a white disc, that was almost the length of his entire body. He gave it a few sniffs before nibbling a bit off the edge.

Pan's eyes almost popped out of their sockets. He dived into the bag.

"Enjoy?" I asked when the crunching had finally stopped. But there was no reply. I peeked into the bag to find Pan curled up inside, fast asleep. I looked back at the book.

While prawn crackers provide all the nutrients a Mini-Dragon needs, eating too much in a single sitting can induce severe tiredness, similar to the phenomenon that affects human beings after a Christmas Dinner.

It's better than him eating my school clothes, I thought. I lifted Pan out of the bag and gently placed him inside my sock drawer.

"Thanks for this, Min," I said, returning to the book.

"No problem. You might as well hang on to it," she said. "Is that where he sleeps then, in your sock drawer?"

"Yeah," I said. "Why?"

"I don't know," she said, looking around the room. "It's just … do you think your bedroom is a good place for him?"

"At first I didn't," I admitted. "After he had a run-in with our cat and then my sister, but now he keeps the door shut and he's fine."

"So he's here all day by himself?" asked Min.

I didn't like Pan being cooped up all day, either, but what else could I do?

"Pan's happy staying here," I said, "and I love having him around. Which other kid has something as cool as a Mini-Dragon to come home to?"

"All right, as long as you know what you're doing," she said, before pointing at a line in the book. "But I think you ought to keep that in mind."

The line read:

> **Despite their size, Mini–Dragons DO NOT make good pets.**

"I didn't think he'd go through all those crackers so fast," said Min as I walked her to the door. "I'll bring some to school tomorrow for you. I'd love to see him again, though."

"Yeah, of course," I said. "Hey, you should come to my birthday party on Saturday. You can keep him amused while I try out my awesome new scooter."

"Sure, I don't mind Mini-Dragon-sitting for a bit," she laughed.

Letting other people know about Pan seemed to have some advantages after all. Maybe I *should* have told... Oh no!

JAYDEN!

I opened the front door for Min just as Jayden was about to ring the bell.

"Where have you been?" he asked. "I was waiting at the park for ages!"

Before I could open my mouth, Jayden clapped eyes on Min.

"Oh, I see what's going on..." he said.

"You do?" I asked, doubting very much that he did.

"Yeah. You've got yourself a girlfriend," he said.

My face went bright red.

Min just laughed. "He wishes," she said.

"No, I don't!" I said. "And no, she isn't."

"That explains why you've been chasing her around the past few days," said Jayden. "You know, you could have told me. I would have been cool with it. I'm supposed to be your best friend, or did you forget that, too?"

He was right, I should have told him.

Not about Min, but about Pan, from the
start. And I would have told him then if he'd
hung around. But after a final, furious look,
he was gone.

CHAPTER 8
UP IN FLAMES

The next day at school, I finally told Jayden everything.

Of course he didn't believe me.

"Seriously?" he said. "That's the best you could come up with? A dragon in your dinner? Give me a break, Eric."

"It's true!" I said. "I can prove it. Tomorrow, at my birthday party, I'll show you. You're still coming, right?"

"Yeah," he sighed. "I'll be there."

After dinner that evening, Pan and I settled down to play some video games. Mini-Dragons really are excellent at them. I lost every game, but I didn't care. Things were finally starting to go right:

1. Min wasn't going to hand Pan over to the government.

2. I now knew what Mini-Dragons ate and had a reliable supplier of prawn crackers.

3. Once Jayden saw Pan he'd know I was telling him the truth.

4. I hadn't heard a peep from Toby.

5. Best of all, tomorrow was my birthday and I would *finally* be getting my Thunderbolt scooter. After all, I was only on Strike Two.

My mind had been so preoccupied that I had barely had time to look forward to my birthday, but now I couldn't wait. Party, cake, Thunderbolt! Maybe all at the same time!

"This is too easy," said Pan, after winning

another game. He put aside his controller.
"Oh, hey, I meant to tell you, I've discovered I
can burp the alphabet."

I sat up straight. Pan had my attention.

"Go on, then," I said.

A small flash of light shot out of Pan's
mouth, along with:

BUUUUUURRRRR-AAAAAAA-PPPPPPPPPP!

Then another blast of fire followed by:

BUUUUUURRRRR-BBBBBBB-PPPPPPPPPP!

Pan wasn't just burping the alphabet – he
was flame-burping the alphabet.

And. It. Was. Hilarious.

BUUUUUURRRRR-CCCCCCC-PPPPPPPPPP!

Well, you get the picture.

I was rolling around on the sofa laughing
when I noticed Pusskin creeping past, heading
for Pan. But she seemed to have a sudden
change of heart when the letter U came
within a whisker of burning off her whiskers.

"Somehow I don't think she'll be bothering you any more," I said through snorts of laughter, as a terrified Pusskin backed away.

"Eric!" shouted Dad from upstairs. "Can you bring up my tactics? I think I left them in the living room."

I grabbed a thick pile of paper from the coffee table.

But just at that moment, Pan burped the letter V...

...which caused Pusskin to panic and bolt towards the door...

...but she smacked straight into the back of my legs instead...

...causing me to fall over...

...flinging the paper into the air...

...right into the path of Pan...

...at the moment he burped the letter W.

The letter W is a tricky letter at the best of

times, so I wasn't surprised that a flame burp
required extra effort.

You can say this for dragon breath – it doesn't just set things on fire. It obliterates them. There wasn't a shred of Dad's tactics left.

"Months of hard work, gone," wept Dad, after I broke the news to him...

The news that I had taken his tactics to school to show everyone but accidentally lost them on the way there. Yes, it was a ridiculous story, but not quite as ridiculous as telling him that a Mini-Dragon that I found in a Chinese takeaway box had accidentally incinerated them while flame-burping the alphabet.

"Well, congratulations, Eric, you've done it," said Dad. "**STRIKE THREE!** No scooter. And the party's cancelled, too."

"We can't cancel the party," said Mum

in her calm yoga voice, making circular motions with her hands while doing the splits. "Everyone's RSVP'd."

Dad looked dumbfounded. "SO?"

"It's short notice – it's the night before!"

"I don't care!" said Dad.

"We've *paid* for everything."

"Ah," said Dad. Mum was finally speaking his language. "Well, in that case, fine, the party still goes ahead. But no scooter. Not now, not ever. Thanks to you, Eric, the Kippers will almost certainly lose tomorrow."

"Yes, Monty," sighed Mum. "*That'll* be the reason."

"Sorry about your scooter," said Pan.

I turned over in bed, ignoring him.

"Did you hear me, Eric?" asked Pan.

"I said sorry. About the scooter? Can you hear me? Has something happened to your hearing?

"Eric?

"Eric?

"Eric?

"Eric?

"Eric?"

"I can hear you, Pan!" I snapped. "I'm trying to ignore you."

"Oh," said Pan. "Why?"

"Why?" I replied. "Because thanks to you the one thing I've wanted for months is probably on its way back to the shops as we speak. That's why I'm ignoring you. Now, leave me alone."

"But it was just an accident," said Pan. "I didn't mean to do it. And you did ask me to do the flame-burping."

I knew Pan was right. It wasn't his fault. But I was so mad about not getting my scooter that I wasn't thinking straight. I knew I'd have to apologize, but I didn't want to do it then. It could wait till the morning.

After tossing and turning for what felt like hours, I finally fell asleep.

CHAPTER 9
BOY LOSES DRAGON

When I woke up the next morning, Pan wasn't there. I checked the sock drawer, unfolding every pair of socks in case he had got himself stuck again. I looked under the bed, in my wardrobe, checked every last inch of my room.

I searched the whole house but couldn't find him.

"Happy birthday, Eric," said Mum at breakfast, balancing on her arms with her legs next to her ears. With a sudden jerk, she flipped up into the air and landed on both feet, giving me a huge hug and kiss.

"'Appy bird-day," said Posy, also demanding a hug.

Even though I was supposed to be in trouble, Mum had made me my all-time favourite breakfast – waffles, bacon, waffles, sausages and waffles. But I was in no mood to eat.

"Thanks, Mum. Is Dad still mad at me?"

"Oh, you know your father, he doesn't hold grudges. Except against football referees."

"Is he at the game now?" I asked.

"Yeah, he left before you were up," she said. "But don't worry, he'll be back in time for the party. Speaking of which, get that down you, I'll need you to give me a hand setting things up."

117

After barely touching my breakfast, I went outside and helped Mum. This mainly involved blowing up balloons and carrying out dozens of plates to the buffet table. At first glance, there seemed to be way more food than you would need for the amount of kids invited. But then I remembered Toby was coming. There were sausage rolls, sandwiches, pizza, crisps, cakes, jelly, biscuits and mini-sausages. Or just sausages if you're Pan. Ha! I'd have to tell him that joke. If I could find him.

Jayden was one of the last to arrive.

"Jayden! You came!"

"Yeah, well, I said I would," said Jayden. He handed me a shiny blue box with an envelope attached to it. I opened the card first. It read: Happy Birthday Eric, From J

Straight to the point, that's what I
liked about Jayden's cards. I tore off the
wrapping paper next and opened the
cardboard box. Inside it was:

A Slug Man action figure in
a box (complete with Slime
Shooter accessory)

A big box of toffees

A Thunderbolt user's manual

A Slug Man T-shirt

"Wow, thanks, Jayden," I said.

Jayden nodded. He started making a show of looking around the garden.

"So, where is he, then, this dragon of yours?" he asked.

I looked away. "Er, well, the thing is ... he's sort of gone missing."

Jayden rolled his eyes. "What a surprise. Oh, look, here's your girlfriend."

Min had arrived. "Happy birthday, Eric. This is for you," she said, handing over a shiny silver package. She held up a brown paper bag. "And this is for— Oh..." She broke off, realizing Jayden was standing there.

"It's all right," I said. "I've told him about Pan. He doesn't believe me, though."

"Oh," said Min. "Well, why don't you just show him?"

"The dragon's not here," said Jayden sarcastically.

Min looked concerned. "Where is he?"

"I don't know," I said. "We had an argument last night... I thought he might just be keeping out of my way, but now I'm starting to worry he might have run off."

"What did you argue about?" asked Min.

I explained to them what had happened with my dad and the scooter.

"That scooter you want," said Jayden. "It's blue, right?"

"*Electric* blue," I corrected. "But yeah."

"Jet black handles?" asked Jayden.

"Yeah, but..."

"And a yellow lightning bolt running up the side?" said Jayden.

"Yes, but I'm not getting it, so can you please stop going on about it," I said.

"OK," said Jayden, pointing behind me. "It's just, I wonder what your dad's planning on doing with that one."

"I er… What?" I said, turning around to see Dad with his Kippers strip on, zipping towards us on a Thunderbolt scooter and grinning from ear to ear.

"Doesn't look that angry to me," said Jayden.

"Eric, we did it!" shouted Dad, throwing his arms around me.

"Did what?" I asked nervously.

"We won! The Kippers actually won a game! And it's all thanks to you."

Have you ever had a moment where it seemed like the whole world has gone mad except you? This was one of those moments. Or maybe I was the one who had gone mad, but either way I had no idea what my dad was banging on about.

"What do you mean, it's all thanks to me?"

Dad slapped Jayden on the back. "Ha! Would you look at him, pretending he doesn't know what I'm talking about."

"What *did* he do, Mr Crisp?" asked Jayden.

"What did he do?" asked Dad. "Why, he only came up with one of the greatest football strategies of all time."

"What's that?" I asked.

My dad waved his hand as if moving it over an invisible pitch. "So there we were, fifteen goals down and it was only half-time. I was looking for my half-time orange in my bag when I found a pile of paper I didn't even know was in there. I took it out and it's got all these diagrams and instructions on it. I quickly realized that they're tactics."

"And you thought they were from me?" I asked.

"Well, it was pretty obvious," he said. "I mean, who else would have felt so bad about destroying the originals to go to all the trouble of writing new ones?"

"Yeah, who else?" I said, looking at Min.

"Though I must say your handwriting certainly seems to have improved. Anyway, since I didn't have any better ideas, I thought, why not give them a try? We finished the game 16–15!"

"You actually won?" I asked.

"Thanks to you," said Dad again. "All this time I thought you weren't interested in football and it turns out you're a tactical genius. I can't believe no one else has ever thought to play with eleven strikers. It makes so much sense when you think about it. Anyway, it's only fair that you be rewarded." Dad handed me the scooter. "Happy birthday."

"Wow! Thanks, Dad!" I cried.

Thanks Pan, more like.

"We have to find Pan," I said. "Right now."

"Where could he be?" asked Min.

"I don't know. He could be anywhere."

"Look..." said Jayden. "I'm not saying I believe you ... but look around. Isn't there something wrong with this scene?"

"What do you mean?" I asked, looking out over the rest of the party.

Dad was busy bragging about his victory. Mum was using her yoga skills to beat everyone at Twister. Kids were running about playing. Then my eyes drifted over to the buffet table and I saw what Jayden meant.

Or, rather, *didn't* see it.

"What is it?" said Min.

"There's a table over there full of crisps, sweets, cake and fizzy drinks," I said.

"Yeah ... so?" said Min.

Jayden checked his watch. "Well, every year, by this time, most of that stuff would already be gone."

"So, what's different this year?" she asked.

Jayden and I looked at each other, then said, "No Toby!"

CHAPTER 10
THE ULTIMATE SACRIFICE

"Pan!" I cried as the three of us burst unannounced into Toby's bedroom. Toby was nowhere to be seen, but Pan was sitting in the middle of the floor, tied to a tiny wooden chair that I recognized from Toby's dolls' house (though Toby hates that name – he insists it's a Toy Mansion).

"Eric!" shouted Pan, looking relieved. "Thank goodness you're here. Mini-Dragons are excellent at staying calm under pressure, but I'm not sure I could take another five minutes of Toby."

"What's he done to you?" I said, clenching my fists.

"Oh, Toby still thinks I'm some kind of toy," said Pan, rolling his eyes. "The more I tell him I'm not, the more impressed he is about how advanced I am. He's tied me to this chair until he can figure out how to switch me off. As my mum used to say, he's not the sharpest claw on the dragon."

Min caught Jayden as he fell over.

"That's a d-d-dragon," said Jayden.

"Mini-Dragon," corrected Min.

"Right, right," said Jayden cautiously.

"You must be Jayden," said Pan. "Nice to finally meet you."

Jayden's mouth opened and closed a few times before he managed to squeak out, "You, too."

"Where is he, Pan?" I said, raising my voice. "Where's Toby?"

"Getting something to eat I think," said Pan. "He likes to eat."

"Like a polar bear likes ice," said Jayden, steadying himself.

"When did Toby dragon-nap you?" asked Min.

"This morning," said Pan. "Just after Eric's

dad had left. I was up all night working on new football tactics, you see—"

"Pan, they worked!" I said, interrupting. "The Kippers won! Dad thought I wrote the tactics and he gave me my scooter."

Pan didn't seem particularly surprised. "Of course they won, Mini-Dragons are excellent at football management."

"But how?" I said.

"I learned how to speak perfect English inside a box of beansprouts on a ship across the ocean. Learning how to get eleven men to put a small ball inside a giant net wasn't that hard. Anyway, I must have fallen asleep before I had the chance to put the notes in your dad's bag. I woke up to the sound of the door opening and I had to sprint out after him. He was almost in his car when I caught up and managed to sneak them in his bag. Then when I was strolling back to the house a huge grubby hand swooped down and grabbed me. The next thing I know I'm here being shouted at to 'do something cool. And make it fiery'."

"I was worried you'd run away," I said.

Pan looked confused. "Why?"

"Because of what I said last night. I'm really sorry, Pan."

Pan looked at Jayden. "Is he always this daft?"

A wide-eyed Jayden looked around as if he couldn't believe a dragon was speaking to him. "Um … yeah, pretty much," he said, finally.

"What?" I said.

"I'm hardly going to run away because we had *one* row, am I?" said Pan. "We're friends, remember. Maybe it's different for humans, but Mini-Dragons fall out with their friends all the time. But it doesn't matter because we know it'll be forgotten about the next day."

"No, humans are pretty much the same," said Min.

"Totally," agreed Jayden.

"So you're not mad?" I said.

"Nope," said Pan.

"Well, for the record, I *am* sorry," I said.

"Apology accepted," said Pan. "Oh, and Eric?"

"Yeah?"

"Would you mind untying me?"

"Oh, yeah," I said.

After a couple of seconds of wrestling with the knot, the string tying Pan to the chair fell to the floor and he sprang free ... only to be snatched out of the air by Toby who had charged into the room like a bull who had just heard there was a sale on red rags across the street.

"How did you lot get in here?" he demanded, his face ready to explode.

"Your mum let us in," said Min.

Toby growled. "Well, get out!"

"Give him back, Toby," I said.

Toby laughed. "You always talk about it like it's real."

"I've told you already—" began Pan, but before he could finish, Toby stuck a sock in his mouth.

"That should shut it up for a minute," said Toby. "Seriously, where's the 'off' switch?"

"I said 'give him back'," I repeated.

"Why should I?" said Toby. "I found him on the street. Finders keepers."

"So you're just planning on keeping him in your toy museum?" asked Min, looking around at all the unopened toys that lined Toby's shelves.

"Those are my collectables," said Toby, beaming with pride. "Mum and Dad always buy me two of every toy – one to play with and one to sell to dumb toy collectors when I'm older for loads of money. And, yeah, he's staying here – 'COS HE'S MINE!"

I took a long, deep breath. I didn't want it to come to this.

"Wait there," I said, leaving the room.

I returned a minute later carrying my birthday present.

"What's that for?" asked Toby.

"A trade," I said. "The dragon for the scooter."

Pan shook his head but I smiled at him. He was worth more than a scooter.

"You idiot, Crispo," said Toby. "I already have *three* scooters. What would I want with another one?"

"You have *three*," I said, "but there are *four* in the set. And this is the one you don't have. I would have thought a collector like you would want the whole set."

Toby stroked his chin, considering it. Then he smirked. "You really are dumb. I'll just make my parents buy it. I don't need yours."

I felt like someone had just let the air out of me. I had been sure Toby would go for my offer.

"Er ... but you won't find one like this in the shops," said Jayden.

"Eh?" grunted Toby.

"Yeah..." said Min. "This one has been modified."

"That's right," said Jayden. "It's souped up, amped up, beefed up. Goes like a Chinese rocket."

"You're lying," said Toby, but his face suggested he wasn't so sure.

"It's dragon-powered," added Min. "One of a kind."

Toby glanced at Pan at the mention of the word "dragon". I smiled as I watched his face twitching as he struggled to decide.

"But if you don't want it…" I said, walking towards the door.

"Wait!" shouted Toby. "I didn't say I didn't want it. Let me think." Toby looked longingly at the scooter, then at Pan, then back to the scooter. I took another step towards the door, then heard a huge sigh.

"Fine," muttered Toby. "It's a deal. Probably saved me a fortune anyway, all that talking it does is bound to drain the batteries."

"What happened to the sock Toby gagged you with?" asked Jayden as we left Toby's house.

Pan shrugged before letting out a little belch.

"You've got a bit of wool in your teeth," laughed Min.

Pan was giddy with excitement as we made our way back to my garden. When we arrived, he let out a tiny gasp as he took it all in. It was just a standard birthday party – balloons, banners and presents – but then I remembered that he had never seen anything like it before. And then I realized that pretty much everything was like that for Pan. He had grown up in a cave, then been shipped across the world on a boat before being delivered to my house in a plastic container. And now he was with me, couped up in my bedroom. His life had been one box after another.

I decided that it was time to open the box and let him see the world. I had no idea how yet, but I would figure it out. It would be hard, but I had help now.

Maybe I could bring him to school...

"Eric, where have you been?" asked Mum, appearing out of nowhere. "What is that?"

She was staring at Pan, who stood motionless on the ground.

"Oh, that's my present to Eric," said Jayden, giving me a wink. "Pretty cool, huh, Mrs Crisp?"

Mum didn't seem so sure. "It looks ... sharp."

"Not for a *nine year old*," said Min.

Mum thought about it for a moment, before nodding. "You're right. It's a lovely present. Right, must go, I think they're about to start a game of Limbo over there without me. Ha! They're in *my* backyard now."

"Nice one, you guys," I said after she

had gone. "And great work on the freezing, Pan."

"Thanks," he said. "I've been practising all week."

Min let out a sigh. "It's great having Pan back and all … but I can't believe that horrible Toby gets to keep your scooter. It's not very fair."

"Yeah, especially with all those awesome modifications," said Pan.

The three of us looked at each other and laughed. "That was just a fib," I said. "It doesn't have any modifications."

"Yes, it does," said Pan. "I made them."

We stopped laughing.

"What?" I asked.

"Well, the other day I found the scooter in the cupboard under the stairs."

"What were you doing in there?" I asked.

"Hiding from Pusskin," said Pan.

"Oh."

"Anyway, I saw it and thought, *I bet I could make that go faster.*"

"Faster?" I repeated.

Pan nodded. "It was easy. Mini-Dragons are excellent at scooter tinkering."

"Is that true?" Jayden whispered in my ear.

"Well … to be fair, he does tend to be excellent at a lot of things. So I guess it probably is true."

The next moment, there was a loud bang. Everyone turned to watch as a round-looking boy soared through the air on an electric scooter before crashing into an apple tree on the other side of the street.

I remembered a warning from the *Encyclopaedia Dragonica*:

…this can lead to them becoming overconfident in their abilities, sometimes with disastrous consequences.

This might be the sort of thing they were talking about.

"Oh my," said Min, looking stunned.

"I know," said Jayden. "Poor Toby."

"No, not that. I just realized, I was the one who delivered Pan to Eric. In the beansprouts!"

"Really?" I said. "*That's* your concern right now?"

As people rushed to help Toby, the four of us quietly headed to the buffet table.

Eventually my scooter would be returned to me and a confused Toby would be sent for a lie-down as he babbled about tiny talking dragons... But for now, I saw no reason to let a perfectly good birthday go to waste.

I remembered another note of caution from the *Encyclopaedia Dragonica*:

Mini-Dragons DO NOT make good pets.

No, I thought, *but they did make interesting friends.*

Chapter 10

Owing to their smaller, and therefore, more vulnerable stature, Mini-Dragons will typically seek out a companion, to whom they will pledge their eternal devotion and loyalty. In some rare cases it has been known for this companion to be not a dragon, but rather a human.

Encyclopaedia Dragonica

WE CAN'T POSSIBLY
STRESS HOW BAD AN
IDEA THIS IS.

LIKE
SERIOUSLY!

THE MINI-DRAGON COOKBOOK

Hello, reader – Pan here! Now that you've finished hearing about how I came to live with Eric, you might be feeling a bit hungry from reading about all that mouth-watering food mentioned in the story. Well, never fear ... because this is your lucky day! As I'm sure you're aware, Mini-Dragons are excellent cooks so I thought it might be nice, as a thank-you for reading my story, to pass along a few of my favourite recipes. Eric insisted on including one, too, but

between you and me it's pretty disgusting, so I won't blame you if you want to give that one a miss. What can I do. He's my friend. Anyway, **bon appetit!**

PAN'S FAMOUS ROASTED GOAT

Ingredients:

One goat (available at your local mountain range)

Cooking directions:

Take a deep breath and blow.

Cooking time:

Five seconds (probably longer if you're not a dragon).

PAN'S PERFECT PRAWN CRACKERS

Ingredients:

One phone (mobile or landline)

Cooking directions:

Pass the phone to your parents and politely ask them to call your local Chinese restaurant and order some prawn crackers for delivery. Alternatively, become friends with someone whose parents own a Chinese restaurant and get them to bring you free ones.

Cooking time:

Depends on traffic.

PAN'S DELICIOUS DIRTY CLOTHES

Ingredients:

Some clothes (unwashed)

Cooking directions:

Find a washing basket. Open washing basket. Eat contents of washing basket. If no clothes are inside, put lid back down and try again at the end of the week.

Cooking time:

One to seven days (depends when washing day is).

ERIC'S KRAZY KETCHUP SANDWICHES

Ingredients:

Two slices of bread
½ bottle of ketchup

Cooking directions:

Pour ketchup on to first slice of bread. Place second slice of bread directly on top of first slice of bread. Eat.

Cooking Time:

Depends if you have a squeezy bottle or one of those glass ones. No more than two minutes though.

Eric agrees to take Pan to school with him — and quickly regrets it...

Pan's relatives come to visit ... via the sewers!

Hungry for more ?
Here's a sneak peek of Eric
and Pan's next adventure...

THERE'S A
DRAGON
IN MY
BACKPACK!

CHAPTER 1

BRING YOUR DRAGON
TO SCHOOL DAY

There's a dragon in my backpack. This is
what I've been reminding myself of all day.

Q. Why is there a dragon in my backpack?

A. Because I'm too nice, that's why!
And because the dragon's right, it's not fair
that he has to stay in my bedroom all day.

Q. Why is there a dragon living in my
bedroom?

A. Oh yeah, sorry, I should explain...

The dragon isn't one of those full-sized, princess-stealing, knight-guzzling dragons that you've probably heard of. For one thing, I'd never fit one of those in my bag. No, he's a Mini-Dragon. Which means he looks exactly like one of those other dragons – same green scaly skin, fiery breath, sharp teeth and claws – except that he's about fifteen centimetres tall and can talk. Oh, can he talk! His name is Pan and here's how he came into my life:

Property developers destroy Pan's home in China.

Pan's parents bundle him in a crate of beansprouts bound for Mexico to stay with his aunt and uncle.

The restaurant in Mexico that ordered
the beansprouts closes down.
The crate is sent to England, to my friend
Min's parents' Chinese restaurant.

Min delivers Pan to my
house in a takeaway
meal without realizing.

I end up with a Mini-Dragon
who gives me no end of grief.

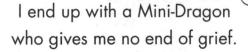

So now Pan spends most of his day in my house playing video games, reading comics and watching TV. Which sounds like a perfect day to me, but for some reason he finds it boring. For ages he's been begging me to let him come to school and last night I finally gave in, on the condition that he keep quiet and stay out of sight in my bag.

ABOUT THE AUTHOR

Tom Nicoll has been writing since he was at school, where he enjoyed trying to fit in as much silliness into his essays as he could possibly get away with. When not writing, he enjoys playing video games (especially the ones where he gets beaten by kids half his age from all over the world). He is also a big comedy, TV and movie nerd. Tom lives just outside Edinburgh with his wife, daughter and a cat that thinks it's a dog.

THERE'S A DRAGON IN MY DINNER!
is his first book for children.

ABOUT THE ILLUSTRATOR

Sarah Horne grew up in Derbyshire and spent much
of her childhood scampering in the nearby fields with
a few goats. Then she decided to be sensible and
studied Illustration at Falmouth College of Arts and
gained a Master's degree at Kingston University.

She now lives in London and
specialises in funny, inky illustration.